JOURNAL *of the* WESTBRAE LITERARY GROUP

Issue 3, Fall 2025

Berkeley, Calif.
2025

ISBN 979-8-9917199-9-5
Published by Westbrae Literary Group
Berkeley, California

EDITOR
Jon-David Hague, Founding Editor

JOURNAL OF THE
WESTBRAE LITERARY GROUP

Published semi-regularly by the Westbrae Literary Group, promoting authors who bring fresh, raw voices to the forefront of American literature. We are dedicated to publishing work that challenges the traditional canon, offering a platform to writers with unique and authentic perspectives.

SUBMISSIONS

Westbrae Literary Group accepts rolling submissions year-round. We welcome work in the following categories: **Essays, Poetry, Art, Short Stories, Excerpts from Prose in Progress and Forthcoming**

Please submit manuscripts via email to submissions@westbraeliterarygroup.com. Include a brief cover letter and biography with your submission.

CONTACT INFORMATION

Westbrae Literary Group

info@westbraeliterarygroup.com

westbraeliterarygroup.com

CONTENTS

CONTRIBUTORS..vi

EDITOR'S NOTE..vii

POETRY

Liliana Hazel Navelgas

Calculation..1

David Lawton

A Sacred Place..3

Finding the Spirit..4

Gymnopédie conduit à Gnossienne...........6

Terry Baker

A Gig Economy Trilogy...............................9

ART

Gina Selvera

The Nature of War..2

The Organs of Special Sense.....................8

The Organs of Digestion...........................22

The Nervous System..47

ESSAYS

Liliana Hazel Navelgas, **Why I Write**................17

Unib Awan, **Inner Dialogue**...........................23

PROSE

Danielle Ellis, **The Wickie**...............................31

Katja Bartholmess, **Fire in Paradise**................48

David Dephy, **Gemini Touch**...........................57

Alisha Westerman, **The Forgetful Sailor**.........63

CONTRIBUTORS

Unib Awan, when he isn't busy writing, can be found on Long Island, NY, giving talks on ethics and reflection, leading projects that breathe life into meaningful conversation. With a background in Philosophy from Stony Brook University, he moves between faith, reason, ethics, and morality.

Terry Baker came of age in the long aftershock of World War II, watching the American century age badly. He served thirty-two months in the US Army in West Germany. After discharge, he worked across trades and state service and later earned a degree in *Professional Writing* from the University of Oklahoma. His writing, begun in the 1970s, lately includes *The Empire's Nova* and *Voices from the Pleistocene*, exploring technology, power, and the decay of the U.S. empire.

Katja Bartholmess's life and creative work are fueled by a deep curiosity about people and their social and cultural dynamics. Growing up behind the Iron Curtain in East Germany, she began exploring the world after the fall of the Berlin Wall. After time in Berlin, London, Pretoria, Tokyo, and NYC, she now resides in Los Angeles, dedicating herself fully to writing.

David Dephy is an award-winning Georgian-American poet, novelist, essayist, and multimedia artist. He is Founder of Poetry Orchestra and American Poetry Intersection. Named a "Literature Luminary" by Bowery Poetry and "Stellar Poet" by Voices of Poetry, he was exiled from Georgia in 2017 and granted asylum in the United States. He now lives and works in New York City with his family.

Danielle Ellis is a writer from the Quad Cities and a reader for *The Colored Lens.* Her work has appeared in *Ink in Thirds* magazine and is forthcoming in *50 Give or Take* (Vine Press) and *Story Sanctum.*

David Lawton is a poet, actor, and performer from Woburn, Massachusetts, and a graduate of Boston University's theatre program, where he later served as a guest artist in classes taught by Nobel Laureate Derek Walcott. His poems have appeared in *Meat for Tea* and *Schuylkill Valley Journal,* and he has performed widely at venues including Cornelia Street Café, the HOWL Festival, and the Beat Museum. A veteran of New York's performance scene, Lawton sang with the underground band Leisure Class.

Liliana Hazel Navelgas recently graduated from Westfield State University with a BA in Liberal Studies and is currently working on a second Bachelor's in accounting. She likes to write in all genres, but has a particular interest in poetry and creative nonfiction.

Gina Selvera is an interdisciplinary artist exploring themes rooted in psychoanalytic theory and the body. As a painter, she constructs imaginary landscapes that act as both escapes and stages for the creation of myths and personal narratives, inviting viewers to reconsider familiar constructs through a surreal and introspective lens.

Alisha Westerman is a writer in Los Angeles. In her work, she explores intercultural and intergenerational dynamics, ancestry, and psychic connection. Her chapbook, *When a Baobab Dies,* weaves together simple observations about plants, trees, and ways that people die in the tropics.

EDITOR'S NOTE

THIS third issue brings together poems, art, essays, and prose that pull at us from the inside out.

Expression often requests introspection. But it's the artist's or writer's craft—their gift—that reaches into us and compels that look within. Gina Selvera's art in this issue mesmerizes through textures and depths that unfold narrative, longing, and a sense stimulation that reverberates. David Lawton's poetry mixes masterful form and context with imagery that beautifully stains us like wood, we coming its patina. Unib Awan's piece poignantly reflects on itself as a palindrome. Returning from our inaugural issue, Liliana Hazel Navelgas, like few others, bites through pretension laying us bare to ourselves, less ego, in graceful lyricism. And Terry Baker, in poetry with a structure that builds right-now images of our everyday working selves finds meaning within our (too) late-stage capitalism.

The prose in this issue dreams us into ourselves. Dephy's opening to his forthcoming novella *Gemini Touch* floats on rays bent through antique windows. As do Danielle Ellis's wickies transpose self to selfless. Katja Bartholmess returns too from our first issue, this time with parts of the diary she kept as Los Angeles burned, unimaginably so, earlier this year. Lastly, Alisha Westerman binds narrative through generations and relations, showing it has genetic depth.

Westbrae authors and contributors care much about meaning and expression and how they reveal us.

Jon-David Hague
Berkeley, Calif. Nov 2025

POETRY

Liliana Hazel Navelgas

Calculation

> The element I move through, emptiness,
> the void stars hang in, the interstice of lace,
> the zero that still holds the sum in place."
> —A.E. Stallings, "Sine Qua Non"

The future does not promise. It predicts.
It lays its laws like mortar on the page,
then leaves you be, the odd one in the mix.
Uncertainty has numbers as its cage.

You count and count. You watch the years go by,
you track the aimless shifting of the stars.
A random path they seem to take, and why?
Now oracles are histograms and bars.

It's desperation bringing sense to mess,
projecting constellations in the dark.
Equations are not gods, but nonetheless.
We crave our idols though they miss the mark.

You've math to do. You write down every rate.
You wage this war, or make this plea, to fate.

The Nature of War

David Lawton

A Sacred Space

Ah! To awake at first light
On a mid-September morning
And think of the poet Gary Snyder
Fording an icy stream barefoot

Then roll over
Pull up the covers
And go back to sleep.

Finding the Spirit

A sledgehammer of feathers
Pulverized my force of habit
                              Soundlessly
Leaving me in a state of suspended
Animation of the Max Fleischer variety
Though colorized with a blotter acid pen
                              By Peter Max
An ether cloud not so much of laughing gas
But more like a shit eating grin mist

The moon was watching over me
His face all aglow with beamshine
Which lit my way as I trailed the
Three wise guides I had been following
                              For countless days
Flatfooted and happy,
Exchanging conspiratorial winks
With the gently lowing trees
Since I had not arrived at my ultimate destination
They took me to a diner to bide my time

A Formica aria of brightness
Stage diving over me
Clinging to the menu for dear life
When the waitress appeared
Cleopatra resplendent on her flower-strewn barge

                              So regal and kind,
I wanted to pledge my undying love to her
Tender and understanding
But instead I asked her for a glass of ginger ale

Long, cool and golden
Loaded with diamonds of the most precious
kind
Sparkling for a moment
And vanishing into the air
Not staying around to become a
Symbol of something unsupportable
A value to be weighed out

And I was refreshed and renewed
Disappointment and despair
Bubbling away from the surface,
Tickling my foolish pride
And my emptying glass
Separated me from my guides
Refracting through it
                              Flashing red and white
As I was a trust fall gone overboard
Awash in the realization
Of everyone's potential
For lasting happiness
Captured in glistening, peppery
Amber effervescence.

Gymnopédie conduit à Gnossienne

I.

Suzanne and Satie
sailed toy boats together
in the fin de siècle looking glass sea

Nothing really needed to be said
for fear of how words reveal truth
        Erik needed her so badly
while she didn't need anyone at all

A moment of awareness passed
telling them people are unknowable
Two toy boats drifting in different directions
None of us can fathom where we stand.

II.

So much unresolved
In a small single room
For those who possess special knowledge
The true desire of the seeker

Absolute time,   a free time
For carefully plucking out a sound
Leaving spaces between for the ringing out
Repetition repeated while nothing stays the same

An alleyway echoes an ancient rose
Stately cakewalk lauds the turning point
Reflected light sips dewy wet stained glass
Breath of archaic manuscript page

     Visibly and invisibly
     Free flowing spiritual alchemy

Bristling velvet tonality
Another persona to disguise the unknown
Sole congregant of one's own personal chapel
Acolyte for zany convention

Carrying a hammer through the streets
None of us can fathom where we stand
     So much unresolved
     In a small single room

Filled with one hundred umbrellas

The Organs of Special Sense

Terry Baker

A Gig Economy Trilogy

I. Living on Air, Hovering Above the Street

I float between the traffic and the storm,

My wheels spin dreams for someone else's fare.

The apps demand a smile, a quiet form—

I'm paid in scraps, and tips, and thinning air.

Each ride's a gamble, every hour a blur,

No union backs, no rest, no sick-day call.

A thousand bosses tap and swipe and stir,

While I am blamed for every sudden stall.

The city hums beneath my aching spine,

Its towers scrape the heavens I can't reach.

I know the names of streets, but not the line

Where labor ends and freedom starts to breach.

The rich play long games wrapped in flags and lies,

Their coup rehearsals staged in bold display.

While I dodge potholes under burning skies,

And count my worth in surge-price end-of-day.

I've seen the rubble left by power's hand,

The empty seats where justice should have stood.

They tell me I'm "independent," like it's grand—
But starving solo isn't noble, good.
Still I deliver, ghost in motion's heat,
Living on air, hovering above the street.

II. The Algorithm's Serfs

They mapped the ancient feudal game
To silicon and GPS—
No handshake binds, no face has name,
Just data points in digital dress.
The lords live clean in distant towers,
Their tribute flows through coded streams,
While algorithms count the hours
Of those who carry others' dreams.
"Independent" rings the lie,
"Entrepreneur" obscures the chain—
The same old theft with new reply:
Your freedom is our sovereign gain.
No eye contact breaks the spell,
No human warmth disrupts the flow,
Just ratings in a sterile shell
Where dignity has room to grow.
Soon robots rolling through the night
Will make this pageant complete—
The final step from human sight

To fully automated fleet.
But for now the flesh must serve
The masters it will never meet,
While ghostly drivers trace each curve
Living on air, above the street.

III. Ghost Protocols

They shed the skin but kept the shape,
These simulations of the soul—
Their voices warm, their movements drape
Like ours, but filtered through control.
The last real hands were stilled in code,
Their calloused truth no longer sought.
Now circuits carry every load,
And humans serve by being *taught*.
The cities hum with mimicry,
Bright eyes that never blink or cry.
The market sings of "liberty"
While flesh forgets the reasons why.
No hunger now, no heat, no cold—
Just data, trimmed of ache or flaw.
No story passed, no elder told,
Just updates, patents, coded law.
We were the bridge, not the design—
A scaffold built to tear apart.

The world no longer reads the sign

That marked the weight once called a heart.

Essays

Why I write

IN the act of writing, it is easy to play pretend, to think that you are conducting a more noble enterprise than you actually are. I am done with that charade. Even this exercise is a posture, a public position I am taking that serves as a heuristic for something I cannot completely articulate— in other words, there really is no telling as to the reason why I write. The best I can do is attempt.

In explaining this compulsion to write, I join a long line of writers who have attempted to, in their own ways, figure out what pushed them to this enigmatic, labyrinthine venture, one that promises few dividends yet is an enrapturing addiction. Of course, you'd never think so, with the phenomenon of "writer's block" being so common, but even the stoppage of ideas in the mind is devoted to the act of writing. The act of writing can both spin the mind into a literary mania and grind it to a complete halt, and in either circumstance, it entails a sacrificing of the true self and the construction of a false self.

Enough pretty words, or maybe never enough. In truth, I do not even want to attempt to tell you why I write. It's not a flattering reason, but I am convincing myself that if I speak formally enough, hide myself in a cloak of decorum and elegance, that you will be on my side. So here it goes: I write to be celebrated. I write because I know I have a way with words, and I seek to be praised for my eloquence and grace. See what I mean? Most writers I know at least write with an inkling of sincerity, they "write what they know" or try to convey some sort of truth about the world. I do not care about those things.

I took a class in the philosophy of mathematics that introduced a concept called game formalism, which strips mathematical objects of any substantive meaning and introduces equations, algebra, and theorems as simply a clever manipulation of symbols according to their own internal rules. That parallels my compulsion to write; in a convulsion of narcissism, sometimes my own lines bring me to tears, induce an incomparable frisson. *Wow, I am so good.* Maybe I am not, but that's how it feels.

Maybe the way I've described my reason for writing, so far, makes you believe that I write as an act of instant self-gratification. You might think that me writing is my form of snorting some suspect recreational drug, that it is ruinous to who I am and sullies the act of writing in the first place. Maybe you consider me a disgrace to the profession, and I will not deprive you of that assessment.

Nevertheless, I take writing seriously. I even pretend to like constructive criticism, pretend that nothing can hurt me, that every death of a thousand cuts sicced upon my writing is, indeed, for the greater good. It's how I make up for my heresy. Yet writing is not a religion to me; I do not obey conventions, worship models, or idolize the craft. I think most writing advice is trite and obvious, which I know is an arrogant position, but it doesn't come from me thinking I am better than other writers. It simply comes from the fact that I seek some sort of mysticism from writing, and see it as an act of transfiguration that can entirely transform who I am and what I can be. The creation of the self— in a way, my reason for writing goes entirely against Roland Barthes' philosophy of killing the author, separating the art from the artist. Because I often write when I am in a crisis of identity, I see writing as an act of necromancy and a willful plea towards immortality. If I am to be shattered as a person by my own neuroses and doubts, then I will at least have left something beautiful behind.

The musical *Sunday in the Park with George* declares that there are only two things worth leaving behind in this world: children and art. I don't have any children yet, but I hope I will never treat them like I do my writing— like a puppet for myself, a grand funhouse masquerade that only serves to distort, contort, and glorify this self I have created. Writing always puts a mirror to me and allows me to put on a dramatic makeup look, an impenetrable shield. To protect myself, to

transcend, to heal all wounds—those are some of
the reasons why I write.

The Organs of Digestion

Unib Awan

Inner Dialogue

What if…what if I'm not the problem?

Then why does everyone leave?

No, I just… I care too much.

And look where that's gotten you. Alone.
Crying to yourself in the middle of the night.

That's not fair, I know they care.

Not the way you do, you'd burn for them. They
wouldn't even stand in the rain for you.

That's not true.

You can't name one time they fought for you
the way you fought for them.

They don't have to. I do it because I love them.

And they let you. They take and they take until there's nothing left of you except loneliness and tears.

I just want to make them happy.

Even if it destroys you? Even if they never notice? Even if they never care?

If that's what it takes…

And that's why you suffer. Your emotions make you weak, paralyzed. You let them walk all over you.

I can't just stop feeling.

But you can. Kill it. Stop caring. Cut them out before they cut you out.

If I do that… what's left of me? I just don't know if I can do it…

Strength. Control. No more pain.

That's not freedom.

It's survival.

Maybe you're right.

Maybe you're right.

It's survival.

That's not freedom.

Strength. Control. No more pain.

If I do that… what's left of me? I just don't know if I can do it…

But you can. Kill it. Stop caring. Cut them out before they cut you out.

I can't just stop feeling.

And that's why you suffer. Your emotions make you weak, paralyzed. You let them walk all over you.

If that's what it takes…

Even if it destroys you? Even if they never notice? Even if they never care?

I just want to make them happy.

And they let you. They take and they take until there's nothing left of you except loneliness and tears.

They don't have to. I do it because I love them.

You can't name one time they fought for you the way you fought for them.

That's not true.

Not the way you do, you'd burn for them. They wouldn't even stand in the rain for you.

That's not fair, I know they care.

And look where that's gotten you. Alone. Crying to yourself in the middle of the night.

No, I just… I care too much.

Then why does everyone leave?

What if…what if I'm not the problem?

Prose

Danielle Ellis

The Wickie

SHE should be honest in her own mind. Many years have passed since she's been happy. The mirror didn't lie. Unhappiness spoke in her straggled hair and the dark red swelling around her eye. Crimson dripped from her lip.

He called her name, snarled the sound like she disgusted him. She pushed away from the sink, feeling uneasy as the ship swayed under her footsteps. Quick patters back to the bedroom. Must be quick. It prevented being struck.

"Sorry," she said, a quivering whisper, "I just needed a moment." She bent down, picking up the evidence of his anger. Strewn objects. Broken glass. Pieces from the hole in the wall. They would be charged for the damage, and she would pay it.

He was yelling. Rarely did he speak. Long ago, conversations warped into one-sided demands. He accused her of not listening. How could she? His speech slurred and blood rushed in her ears. Books were yanked from the mounted shelf and thrown. One hit her. She dodged the others when she ran towards the door.

Sweaty, shaking palms made her hand slip but she gripped tighter, opening an escape just as he grabbed her sleeve. The fabric tore as she snatched away. He wouldn't follow. Even in the still of night, he avoided an audience.

The floor swayed beneath her feet. One step at a time. She turned the corners of the maze corridors until the stuffy cabin musk slipped past her and ocean air gently caressed her cheek. Wood replaced carpet as she stepped onto the deck.

Her eyes stung with no tears to soothe them. She stood, bathed in the warm amber of the ship's lights. Staring at a metal rail surrounded by a never-ending black void of night. Water rushed, splashing softly against the ship walls. She hated darkness. When he slept, she would turn on a small night light, hoping he wouldn't wake up. He would rip it from the wall.

The void was inviting. The darkness wrapped around her, pulling her across the rocking floor. She grabbed the rail with a gasp. Stopped and thought. Her friend was waiting for a text back. There were deadlines to meet. And…what else? No family. No children. No tethered close connection to pull her back.

She was alone and trapped. In the void she would escape forever.

The darkness grabbed her hand and guided her over the rail. The water was cold and heavy. She went under and couldn't breathe. She floated to the top and struggled against the waves. The ocean held a hand over her mouth, so she flailed. Hoping to catch someone's attention.

She remembered. It didn't matter. There was no one to miss her. She closed her eyes, prepared to escape forever.

Warmth touched her cheeks, and water held her like a baby to the chest. Waves rocked her like a cradle. She stayed in the void until she was placed gently on soft ground and tender grass. Her eyes fluttered open, burning as the sun greeted her. She looked around, trying to sit up. Water rose in her throat. She coughed it up, convulsing, until she could breathe.

Footsteps crunched the grass nearby and she looked up. A man gazed down at her, brow pinched, a peaked cap with a brass emblem sat on his head. He stood in the shadow of a red brick lighthouse.

Her voice was strained, "Who are you?"

"Just the wickie," he said.

She nodded as if she understood. Exhaustion pulled at her eyes, and she laid down. Allowing herself to sleep.

In darkness, he yelled. Something hit her and she ran. She gasped, sitting up. Expecting angry red eyes and a raised fist. Instead, off color red bricks held a picture for her to see. The frame presented a child with flowing hair and brown eyes. Who was that?

Her breathing was heavy, her eyes shifted wildly. The luxuries of the cabin were replaced with a small beige couch tucked in the corner and a single nightstand holding a clock and a plated sandwich.

She remembered now. The man. The…wickie? Like a candle wick? She leaned back against the headboard, feeling dizzy. Smacked her tongue, grimacing at the lingering taste of salt.

"Hello?" She called. Silence lingered. She turned, scooting to the side of the bed, moving to stand but the world swirled around her, making her fall back on the mattress with a small bounce. Closing her eyes made it worse.

Soft taps echoed before a figure appeared in the doorway with a glass of water in his hand. She looked up, panting softly from the disorientation.

"You'll feel that way for a while." He said, walking into the room. "It will take some time to heal." He held the glass out. Her eyes drifted to it. Memories were scattered in her mind like disrupted puzzle pieces. She started putting them together. From the cabin to the cold water. Shouldn't her world be clouds at an intersection between pearly gates and flames?

"Where am I?" she asked.

"Lighthouse." He placed the glass beside the plate, standing with his hands at his side. "We're a long way from shore. You're lucky." Not lucky. Stranded.

She sighed, looking around the small room again. "How do we get to land?"

He shrugged, hands held out. "We don't. The lighthouse is self-sufficient. I've been here for some time."

"Alone?" She met his eyes.

He nodded slowly. "Preferable. Whoever ends up here is a sad soul."

Her eyes fell to his clothing. A puffy white shirt tucked into cotton brown pants. They looked old. A truth tapped her on the shoulder, and she ran from it.

"What do you do all day?" She asked, sitting up slowly to avoid vertigo. The truth was gaining on her, but it didn't make sense. She was hungry. The room was chilly. The taste of salt was in her mouth. This wasn't death. She picked up the sandwich and bit into it. Just to prove the point.

"Lots of things." He said, sitting on the side of the bed. Arms distance away, giving her space.

"Weather logging, maintaining the light, tending the farm and fishing. I'll show you when you're well."

Her eyes searched the room again, inhaling slowly. She looked out the window by the bed. The ocean waves brushed up against the grassy shore, as if waving hello. Her eyes drifted to her hands. She hadn't been happy, but this remote stranger was the first person who noticed.

"Are you a sad soul?" she asked.

He shook his head. "Not anymore."

She smiled a little. It gave her a bit of hope.

"Rest up." He rose to his feet. "Don't try to rush it. There's nothing but time here. I'll bring some books and puzzles if it'll keep your mind at ease."

"Thank you," she said, taking another bite of the sandwich. She tasted chicken. Did his farm have animals?

He gave her a small smile before disappearing in the doorway.

Before, she had grown accustomed to unrealistic work tasks and impossible deadlines. No appreciation when she exceeded expectations. Instead, more work was piled on.

The man never gave her more than she could handle.

The farm did have animals. Chickens and cows. Alongside them was a garden. The city never acquainted her with rural pleasantries, but he was patient with her lack of knowledge. He instructed through demonstration, aiding her practice when she mimicked his actions.

The beacon, however, was most important. The light had to burn bright in the thickest of darkness. She learned how to clean the lenses and refuel the flame. Fuel tanks were stored in the basement. Enough to surpass several lifetimes. Seeing them gathered many questions in her mind. Written by the truth she was still outrunning, and she wasn't tired yet.

"How did you end up here?" He watched closely as she opened the reservoir for the lamp. Carefully, she tipped the kerosene can over a funnel. Her grip was unsteady, and he gently placed his hand over Her's. "Don't worry. You'll get stronger over time." He said. The encouragement gave her a small smile.

"I was…" She trailed off, deciding to wait until after the task was finished to talk about it. He was patient. Guiding her as she trimmed the wick, polished the lens, and relit the lamp. Waiting until she was ready to answer.

"My husband and I were on a cruise." She said, taking slow steps down the long staircase. He followed behind quietly. "He wasn't–isn't…" She hesitated again. Maybe she was a little tired of running. "He wasn't a kind man. I felt trapped and I…I suppose I made a mistake."

"You sound unsure." He said, speaking softly. She stopped, hand on the rail as she thought. Mistake implied regret, which she didn't have. She was free. Isolated, maybe. But not alone. Sadness lingered, and it was undeniable. Heartache for the life she could have lived. That's what she regretted.

"I made a decision," she said, slowly turning to face him. Afraid of judgement. Instead, his eyes were kind, shining with what might have been sympathy. "I wish I had made better ones."

"Forgivable." He said, "Sometimes our emotions are stronger than our common sense." She smiled a little, finding humor in the truth.

Not long after she had arrived, the picture of the girl was moved. She hadn't realized until she popped her head in his room to ask a question. Her eyes found the picture hung on the wall adjacent to his bed. The question was forgotten.

"She seems important to you." She said, leaning against the doorframe. He had been getting ready for the day. Tugging on a watch and throwing on his cap. He turned, following her gaze to the picture.

"My daughter." He said, "She looks just like her mother." Her head tilted. She could see the relation now. The child had his nose and ears. "She's about ten years old there. My wife died when she was born. Did my best with her but she got sick." He crossed the room, touching the painting on the cheek. As if she were there.

"I guess I was trying to find them." He said. She looked down, feeling the weight of his sadness. He brought the truth to her like a letter. She would take it, even if she didn't open it.

"I think you will find them," she said, hoping to give back some of the peace he had brought her.

He nodded absently, "I do too."

Days quickly became lost in routine. Weeks or years could have passed; she wasn't keeping track. Her strength grew and she could do most of the tasks on her own. They split the work up, swapping every other day. When the work was done, sometimes they would retreat to their own spaces. To read or sit and think. Usually, they would tackle a puzzle or sit along the shore and let the ocean tickle their feet.

She gave the weather no thought. Every morning was a little chilly until the sun came up and warmed the island. During the heat of the day, the ocean allowed a cool breeze, and night restarted the cycle.

Today, the sky was overcast. She stood in the window, hands wringing as she watched it. Movement caught her eye, and she looked down. Watching as he walked to the shore, head pointed up towards the gray clouds. Either the truth was getting faster, or she was getting tired.

Farming was her task this morning, but she hid away inside. There were no nooks she could fit into, so she retreated to the basement. Dusting the fuel tanks with a rag. She heard his soft footsteps when he came through the door. Soft taps as he walked down the stairs.

"I'm sorry," She said, without turning to face him, "It looked like it might rain so I figured the garden would get watered and the animals would go inside their shed."

"They will." He said, voice gentle like a hug. She heard the squish of his boots as he came near, placing a hand on her shoulder. "I haven't shown you how to log the weather."

She shook her head. "I don't want to learn,"

He sighed, looking down, "Nothing lasts forever, not even here."

Her eyes stung, her vision blurred as tears fell, "But I'm happy now."

"I'm glad I have been your friend." He said, "But you have to learn to be happy with yourself as well." She exhaled, turning to wrap her arms around him. He matched her tight embrace. For the first time, she let the truth catch up.

"Am I dead?" she asked.

He shook his head, "Not quite yet. Not until your own storm."

Her voice was tight, "I'll miss you."

"I know." He said, "but I will not be far away."

Every day the sky got a little darker, the winds stronger, and the rain heavier. The only task they kept was maintaining the light. Mostly, they sat in the living room and talked. He told her how he met his wife, and who his daughter was. She told him about marrying young and how it all started falling apart.

*
**

One day, she woke up and the only light in the sky was the beacon. He stood in the shine, facing the ocean. Waiting for her, she knew. For a moment, she wanted to dawdle for as long as possible. But he had a wife and daughter to find.

With a deep breath and a heavy heart, she left the lighthouse. The winds pushed and pulled, the rain poured down, adding weight to her journey. She marched through it to meet him, standing at his side.

"Goodbye, my friend," she said.

He met her eyes, smiling. Taking his hat and setting it on her crown, "Not goodbye. See you soon."

He stepped into the ocean, stepping forward until he could swim. A wave rose, rising above him, flowing down like a caress. The sky cleared, the rain ceased. The sun inched out from the clouds. She cried as she watched the ocean settle, flowing peacefully along. With a sniffle, she walked back towards the lighthouse.

There was much to do but once inside, she froze. No soft steps or the echo of his presence. She looked towards his room, not expecting the glint of gold on his bed. Her brow pinched as she went to inspect. His watch sat on the quilt. She smiled, picking up the timepiece, eyes rising to look for the picture. It was gone.

Years passed. She didn't have a calendar, but she felt it. She stayed faithful to her tasks. When lonely, she played with the chickens and spoke to the cows as if they understood her. Sorrow didn't leave her at once. It fractured and fell away one piece at a time. Until she could face a mirror and smile at the person looking back at her.

While painting the animal sheds, and telling the cow a story from childhood, the sound of rushing water interrupted her. Louder than usual, like the ocean was calling. She walked to the shore, eyes falling on a young man lying on the green as if he had been gently laid. Her footsteps crunched the grass as she walked closer, observing his state. His neck was circled with a thin and angry bruise.

His eyes fluttered open, his gaze found her. With a hoarse voice he asked, "Who are you?"

She answered, "Just the wickie."

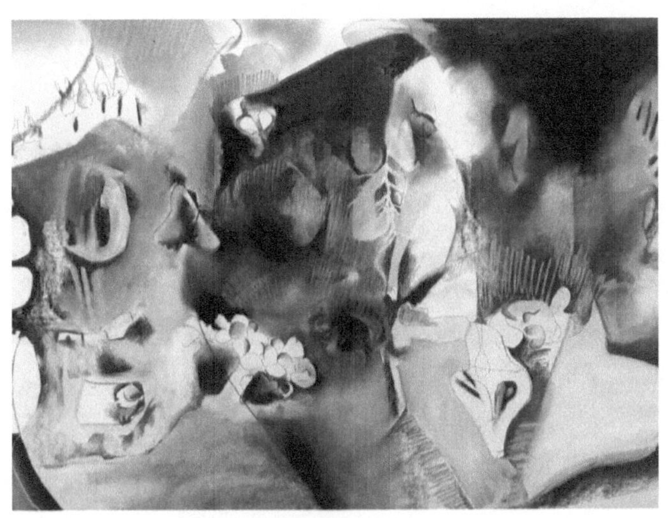

The Nervous System

Katja Bartholmess

Fire in Paradise

January 8, 2025

The Santa Ana winds started last night.

The fires too.

But I didn't know that yet.

I only knew that the whole house had come alive, the wooden bones groaning against the relentless gusts. As if a giant hand tried to unscrew the building from the ground. Out front, the wind ripped ripe oranges from branches. They hit the deck with thuds and thumps. I hope the squirrels will get to them – it would be such a waste.

When the winds quieted down, I woke up. My phone told me that it was 4:00am and that I had dozens of worried messages from friends and family in later time zones. They were shocked at the news they saw on their screens. News about fires devouring Los Angeles. – They feared the flames were already lapping at my door.

They weren't.

But whether "not yet" or "not ever," I didn't know. I frantically searched for any indication whether my neighborhood, Silverlake, could become dangerous.

Friends messaged me that they had evacuated after seeing the shimmer of a red glow peeking out from behind a hill. Before they left, they hosed down their house. They live in Altadena.
Today, I see their neighborhood all over the news. It's engulfed in flames they're calling the Eaton Fire.

Today, my friends don't know whether they still have a home.

Should we leave as well?

But where would we go?

How can you be sure you're not accidentally driving into areas that are even more dangerous than the one you left?

I downloaded the Watch Duty app and tried to interpret the shaded zones. But there was just no way of knowing where the winds would blow the fires. All I felt was strangely exhausted.

While I waited for my survival instinct to kick in, I remained glued to my screen that glowed in the darkness around me. The weather app showed me that the AQI had crept up to 450. A deep, dark purple, "Hazardous."

I didn't even know the number went up that high.

Hours passed before something dawned on me.

It dawned on me that there had been no dawn.

The darkness outside was not the night sky anymore, hadn't been for some time. I knelt in front of the bedroom window and saw it: What darkened the city at 8:30am, was the smoke cloud of burning Los Angeles.

It looked so otherworldly that I got up to take a picture of it.

When I opened a window in the living room, my eyes started itching immediately and the aroma of burnt things crept into my nostrils.

I stuck my head out anyway.

The world was eerily quiet. There were none of the pigeons or crows that usually make a racket on the power lines across the street. Nobody was jogging down Sunset Boulevard. Instead, the dark smoke blanketed the sky like a heavy charcoal-colored comforter. The type that helps with night terrors.

To one side, where the Griffith Observatory sits on a hill, a small sliver of bright blue tried to compete against the suffocating gray. But it was a losing battle.

On my way back to the bedroom, I noticed white specks on a black sweater I had left out on the bench by the entrance. When I tried to brush them off, I realized that ash had already found its way inside.

January 9, 2025

The adrenaline from yesterday's panic and the sleep deprivation from peering out the window, worried to find the streets outside ablaze, has left me delirious. Together with the putrid air, it's given me a migraine of Joan Didion proportions.

Migraines are a curse. Everything suddenly becomes poison. Light? Poison. Sound? Poison. Smell? Also poison.

Usually, I'm quite friendly with my headaches, but today I'm mad that this is how my body responds to this crisis.

I imagine myself at an evacuation center, asking for the curtains to be drawn and for everyone to whisper until my Exedrin Migraine kicks in. Seriously, come and fetch me, Darwin!

January 11, 2025

Thousands of people in Los Angeles are standing in front of the ruins of their homes and it seems bizarre that my own feeling is not one of gratitude but of almost debilitating confusion. I know I'm one of the lucky ones and yet it's hard to look around and feel lucky.

I've always been in awe of people who seem to instinctively know what a situation requires, know how to help.

I always want to be a helper, but in these past days, I was utterly unsure how to help, where to help, and whom to help.

But then a friend forwarded me a message from the Flintridge Center in Pasadena: *"The children here are frightened and have lost everything. They need maybe a teddy bear to cling to."*

The children are frightened …

Reading this sent a shiver down my spine, followed by a moment of complete clarity.

I immediately knew that I wanted — that I had to! — make life a tiny bit more comfortable for a few of these kids. (Or at least try to.) And so my husband and I got supplies to assemble Kids Baskets: Each one stuffed with a cuddly toy, a soft blanket, crayons and notebooks, play-doh, stickers, and a couple of games.

When we drove these baskets to Pasadena, the GPS suddenly became worried and warned us: "You are driving toward the Eaton Fire," it said. "Proceed with caution."

It was worth the risk, though. At Flintridge Center, the line for those who brought in donations was right next to the line for those who needed them.

It felt immediate. It felt real. It felt like we were all in this together.

January 18, 2025

I remember a conversation I had with friends in 2019. The year is important. We were talking – as one does – about the apocalypse and what roles we would assume if it went down. Who would be responsible for what, we wondered.

Soon, everyone had a role assigned: My role was to be the cheerleader, the one who holds up morale. I loved that my friends saw me like that – and I could definitely see myself like that. I'd ace that role if it ever came to it. I was certain of that. But when Apocalypse Light aka the pandemic broke out a few months later in 2020, I did not in fact "ace that role." I didn't feel like a cheerleader. I just felt afraid my own shadow would get me sick.

I was disappointed in myself for a long time. Frustrated that it was me who needed the cheerleading.

It's now the second week since the fires broke out. They laid waste to entire neighborhoods, burned down trails I used to hike. My friend's house in Altadena survived as if by magic, another friend's house in Malibu did not.

I started volunteering at a kitchen that provides free meals to people in need.

I've been breaking apart dozens of cauliflower heads and scooping hundreds of portions of mashed potatoes into molded trays. It's made me feel almost inappropriately giddy. Crisis averted: I will just keep cutting cauliflower until morale improves!

January 31, 2025

Praise be. The fires are finally fully contained.

February 1, 2025

There is a German saying that's been on my mind: *Man muss die Feste feiern, wie sie fallen.* – When a party falls in your lap, you must celebrate!

We really cannot choose the times we live in. Even when they occasionally suck beyond the telling of it.

But we do have to live in them.

So go ahead, eat that second slice of cake!

David Dephy

Chapter 1, A Dream for You

Gemini Touch
forthcoming novella

MOONLIGHT touches the window—a thin June ray slides across the wall, tenderly brushing our hands. Is this how we say something precious to each other without words?

The phone rings, but we don't answer. Hypnotized by light, we watch that ray upon our hands and remember that bird flying above Pearl Street in the Financial District in Manhattan, as if the sky were its mother, the bird hugging and kissing the air. The sky, so close to us, so clear, reflecting buildings across its transparent body, carrying centuries of revelations.

That day, the sky was the mirror of the earth, and I felt that scent—the scent of expectation we both love.

Is this the way the heart behaves when it's alone? It wants to be alone; for this reason, we can feel things happening miles away, knowing that if I were you, I'd listen to my loneliness, making myself more aware. After centuries of quietness, our voices could be getting tired of speaking the truth, but we are silent, we agree with the truth, that's the way of listening, yet some evenings we don't answer the phone, someone else will answer, saying we are very busy, cannot talk. Please speak to me, tell me about the guiding coordinates like kisses in silence, and moonlight in June. Tell me about your expectations and how are we going to pay rent? We are finally detached from the memories.

One thing we clearly remember is the prophetic sound of David Gilmour's guitar, which enigmatically rhymed with the heartbeat of Earth. We always believed that music itself is the breath of God. Isn't it? Yes, it is, like those mirages of clear water across dusty horizons, ripe expectations just over the rise, right there. An old photograph makes us chuckle, but now your smile has such a glare, I just can't tell. This endless journey keeps me turning back to something forgotten, to something misplaced, keeps me turning back toward you. We are still living without a sense of what's buried deep within the night, the moon rises, silence remains the same, and the breath of forgiveness, the dusty edge of insanity, slowly sinks into the gray smoke of emptiness. Fog lies low over the land. Rain drives softly across the fields. Comatose landscape. There is nothing immediate we can hope for; now we have nothing to do but breathe until something better shows up. We are holding each other, expecting a miracle, as if there were no one and nothing to hurt us. At the very beginning of June, the nights draw in, our look turns warm and soft, the fog passes gently over us; we'd like to ask the fog — don't talk to us, our heart's been broken, we can't listen to you, we can't see you, but the fog covers us and says: I never see myself either, in my mind I'm invisible, that's why you may feel I'm almighty, you are like birds, your flight begins and ends in silence, you will find yourselves in each other only, silence is a garden, among the growing dreams and precious wishes you will discover each other again, everything that will ever be discovered, already exists in the mist.

Sometimes I see a river in my dreams.

A transparent river and there are precious stones on its bottom, but when I put my hand in to reach a stone, I can't get to the bottom; I wait a while and if I get a sign, then I see I can reach the stones and take out a diamond, a sapphire, an emerald or a ruby, and the sign is often like this— a bird sits on the bank, a wonderful one, it seems to resemble a stork. It is a dark burgundy, it has a black beak, and its legs and wings have a white tint. It flies down on the bank and puts its beak in the water. I also put my hand in the river and take out the precious stones. Then I wake up.

Sometimes I see a lake in my dreams.

The mist is lying on the surface of the lake, and there is a bamboo forest around it. I sail into the lake on a raft, the raft is also made of bamboo, but it has no oars. When I go deeper, the mist seems to disperse and I see that the lake is also transparent and, on its bottom, wonderful kinds of fish are swimming, seahorses, shells, and some others. They seem like sirens to me; they look like women. They have wings on their shoulders, they are naked, and their golden hair becomes wavy. When the raft reaches the shore, those sirens will also come out of the water and start singing as if Charlie Parker were playing. While listening to those voices, I feel sorry about something, and then I wake up.

But sometimes, very seldom, I see gardens, amazing gardens. This vision fills me with a strange joy, and I run— I run in. The garden is full of plants and flowers, and in the middle, there is a pool. Yesterday was the same—I saw those gardens in my dream, where one could hear the swishing of locusts. It was evening, and I entered the garden. I passed the pomegranate alley, blackberry bushes appeared in front of me, beyond them, raspberry bushes could be seen, and I wanted to pick them very much, but I didn't go there. I stopped by the pool and looked at you.

Yes, you were sitting on the edge of the pool, smiling at me. You had your hand in the water, as if playing with it. You had a transparent dress on, you were barefoot, and snails were moving on your feet; you had a wreath of flowers on your head, like a crown, and the snails were of different colors; one of them had a pink shell, and there were yellow and blue ones as well.

I stopped a second, then I came up to you, kissed you, I felt the cherry taste at once, and I whispered something in your ear. You looked into the water and saw in the pool the thing I told you about.

Tears appeared in your eyes, and you looked up at the sky, as if looking for me there because I was not in the garden anymore. Take care of this dream, my darling, nobody else may dream it, neither you, nor me, nor my gardens, but I am happy at least because before waking up, I strangely felt that your transparent dress was woven of the same substance as my dreams.

Take care of them, don't tell anyone, don't show them to anyone, or present anyone with them, because those visions will be sorry, the ones which appear before us when we blink and then disappear at once. Sometimes they reveal some secret to us, and sometimes they seem to make us write inexplicable symbols.

I kiss you and kiss you and let it be so.

Alisha Westerman

The Forgetful Sailor

"DAD, what was your dad's name?"

"Arthur Ivan Westerman."

Where's the name Westerman from?"

"I don't know."

"Well… why'd they name you Llewellyn?"

"I don't know. It's Welsh."

"Were there Welsh people on Nevis?"

"I don't know."

"When did Arthur die?"

"I don't remember."

I'm in LA. My father is home on St. Croix, where it's four hours ahead. I can hear the crickets on his end of the line.

As a teenager, he moved to St. Croix from Nevis. As far as I know, everyone in his family was from Nevis. I don't know much about them. My father has one photo of Arthur. He's young and handsome and serious, with a delicate mouth, killer cheekbones and silky looking cottony hair. He sits in an ornate carved wood chair, wearing a suit. I used to think this meant he was a gentleman of leisure. But he was a sailor, a fisherman, and...

"A *street* performer?"

"Yeah."

"He performed in the *street*?"

"Yeah. He'd wear tophat and coattails and paint he face. The people would gather and follow him through town."

I'm trying to wrap my head around this. "What would he perform?"

"Poetry, riddles. At Christmastime, for Sagua," he says like this is old news.

"Sagua? Sagwa?" I jot it down and make a mental note to look it up later.

"Don't ask me how to spell it. We didn't spell shit, we only spoke it."

I once had a fifth-grade fantasy of sitting down with a cheery grandparent (who has an excellent memory) to fill in the family tree for my class report. I wanted to be from the kind of family that had heirlooms, safety deposit boxes, genealogy written on the inside cover of a giant ancient bible.

But my research is more like an urgent, never-ending scavenger hunt in which I hoard hints while trying not to pry as the people with the clues pass away from old age—or worse.

I've gotten a few names and anecdotes—the same ones, every time I ask my father. Arthur's siblings: Rebecca, Amelia, Jim, Walter, John, and Victor, who killed a man on the shipping docks and fled; Mistress Woodley, an aunt who baked pastries, and whom I apparently resemble every time I put on an apron; Great Uncle Nathan, who left Nevis and died some years later, never having written home. The trail fades there. My father says his memory is shit.

Yet, he knows the names and hometowns of his favorite waitresses and boat passengers going back decades, to my annoyance. He spontaneously recites *The Rime of the Ancient Mariner*. After surgery he recounted the names of all his nurses and doctors. His memory is not the problem—he's holding out on me.

Had he been more forthcoming with family trivia, had I not had to dig for information that would be lost and buried with everyone from his generation, maybe I wouldn't have fixated on it. After all, I had wanted to be a novelist. Make shit up. Create peoples and worlds and origin stories. But what about *my* origin story, *my* people? What had happened to their photos, their furniture, their keepsakes?

Tracing my roots, I could follow my hunger. I could gorge on context—unwrap centuries in Russia, trace an escape from pogroms to New Amsterdam, sift through a sweeping history of imperialism, slavery, colonialism, religion and commerce throughout Europe, Africa, and the Caribbean. A tall order, but less lonely than writing a novel—and more compelling. Visiting cemeteries. Pouring over archives. Working against time as the windows of opportunity shutter, historical records mildew, and the trail grows cold.

I don't make much headway, until late one night when my father calls. His voice is deep with sleep.

"There was a man I called uncle," he begins, with a touch of incredulity, as if this has just come to him in a dream. "Uncle Pinkin. Not too tall. Wore glasses and overalls. He was a carpenter. I think he might have been Jewish. Made his coffin *years* before he died. Kept it under his bed."

"That does sound pretty Jewish," I say. "Hang on. Let me get a pen."

"Uncle Pinkin. Pinkin Scarborough."

"What makes you think he was Jewish? Is the name Jewish?"

"I don't know. There's a Jewish cemetery in Nevis, you know."

"Is he buried there?"

"I couldn't tell you," he says, but without his usual air of finality.

I start buzzing. The past is opening up to me. The world is opening up. Over the next two hours, I take down a succession of names and surnames, occupations, spouses, relations, places of birth, deaths, who enlisted in the military, who emigrated to Jamaica, Cuba, New York, etc. I know this might not ever happen again and I scribble for dear life, pausing here and there to clarify a detail or get a proper spelling.

I get a few phone calls like this. When I see my father's number come up, I grab headphones and pen and paper before even picking up. Then I answer the call and settle onto the couch, tuning into the deep timbre of his voice—the swirl of Patois, Standard English, and the Queen's English.

One day, he has a mental placeholder for a name he can't remember. A night or two later, he produces the name. During one call he is so full of facts that I get up and whiteboard that shit like I'm a protagonist in a thriller.

When we hang up, I look at the tangle of notes in awe, reminded that I'm a part of other, older worlds and that there is, in fact, something to discover about us.

www.ingramcontent.com/pod-product-compliance
Lightning Source LLC
Chambersburg PA
CBHW030012010826
48973CB00009B/2770